Custer's
Last
Battle

RED HAWK'S ACCOUNT OF
THE BATTLE OF
THE LITTLE BIGHORN

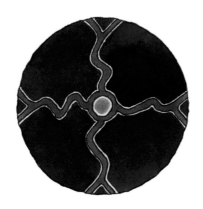

Crazy Horse

Custer's Last Stand
Troops F, C and E

6

Troops I and L

5

Cheyenne

Black Moon

Custer's retreat

Gall

Eastern
Sioux

Sans Arcs
Sioux

Deep Coulee

Muskrat Creek

4

Miniconjou
Sioux

Little Bighorn River

Blackfeet
Sioux

Oglala
Sioux

Hunkpapa
Sioux

Gall

Crazy Horse

2

N

1

Reno's 2nd. position

Reno's 1st. position

Reno's advance

0   1   2 miles

Custer's Last Battle

RED HAWK'S ACCOUNT OF
THE BATTLE OF
THE LITTLE BIGHORN
JUNE 25, 1876

Told & Illustrated by
Paul Goble

Foreword by
Joe Medicine Crow

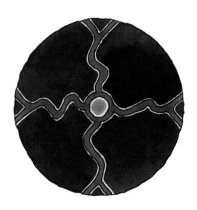

Wisdom Tales

Custer's Last Battle: Red Hawk's Account of the Battle of the Little Bighorn
© Paul Goble, 2013

Wisdom Tales is an imprint of World Wisdom, Inc.

Wisdom Tales wishes to thank the South Dakota Art Museum for their assistance in the loan
and scanning of the original artwork of this title.

Custer's Last Battle is a revised and updated edition of Red Hawk's Account of Custer's Last
Battle, © Paul and Dorothy Goble, 1969, published by Macmillan, London and Pantheon Books,
New York; and Bison Books, © Paul Goble, 1992, University of Nebraska Press, Lincoln.

Cover: Original painting by Paul Goble

Library of Congress Cataloging-in-Publication Data

Goble, Paul.
  Custer's last battle : Red Hawk's account of the Battle of the Little Bighorn, June 25, 1876 /
told & illustrated by Paul Goble ; foreword by Joe Medicine Crow.
     pages cm
  Includes bibliographical references and index.
   ISBN 978-1-937786-11-3 (hardcover : alk. paper) 1. Little Bighorn, Battle of the, Mont.,
1876--Juvenile literature. I. Title.
  E83.876.G56 2013
  973.8'2--dc23
                                                                        2013010123

Printed in China on acid-free paper
Production Date: April 2013; Plant & Location: Printed by Everbest Printing (Guangzhou, China),
Co. Ltd; Job / Batch #:111859

For information address Wisdom Tales,
P.O. Box 2682, Bloomington, Indiana 47402-2682

www.wisdomtalespress.com

Foreword

I am now 98 years of age, so I was alive to meet many survivors of the Custer battle. I talked directly with the Cheyenne, Arapaho, Sioux, and the Crow scouts who were at the battle. My grandfather, White Man Runs Him, was a Custer scout at the battle. His Crow name really means "Chased by a White Man," given to him because the soldiers never caught him. The Indian scouts warned Custer of the danger but he ignored them and attacked the Sioux-Cheyenne camp.

Custer came to fight and try to end the Indian way of life. The Sioux condemned Custer for invading their country, so we say that they "Siouxed him" for it. It's funny, yes? Custer and his men got Siouxed.

There are over 3,000 publications about the Custer battle. But most of them ignore the accounts of the only survivors of the battle. The Indians knew the story, but most historians don't want to listen to them. My people did not depend on writing, so they had very good memories of events. Everyone should know the true story of the battle, so I wrote a reenactment in the form of a pageant: "Battle of the Little Bighorn Reenactment". It is historically accurate.

The Little Bighorn Reenactment is held every year on the third week of June. Hundreds of people participate on horseback to recreate the battle, including many Crow Indians. It is exciting to watch. The Reenactment is located just south of Crow Agency, Montana. It is between the historic places of Custer's Last Stand Hill and Reno-Benteen Battlefield.

Paul Goble's retelling of the Custer battle is also based on Indian sources. It is very accurate. So you can also learn the real story from this book.

Paul Goble is a good friend. I have known him for many years. He sure can draw! His paintings are accurate in all the details. They bring the story of the Custer battle to life.

Joe Medicine Crow

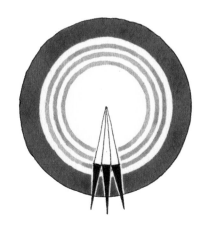

Author's Introduction

In this special edition of my first book, *Red Hawk's Account of Custer's Last Battle* (1969), it needs to be restated that the account is fiction, but told in the manner of the published accounts of Indian people who had taken part in the battle (see the References on the last page).

It is easy to look back at one's early work and to be embarrassed by its innocent beginnings and its mistakes. One has to start somewhere, and in order to make a start it is necessary to be influenced, to be excited and to love something passionately. Readers who know the literature will recognize my influences: the echoes of *Black Elk Speaks* by John G. Neihardt are plain, and the style of ledger-book art in my illustrations is obvious. Forty-three years later, and having written and illustrated almost as many books, I still love those books which influenced me so greatly. In time I gradually found my own style of writing, and other ways to draw and paint. This included the addition of the flora and fauna of the Great Plains, which as an amateur naturalist, is my other passion in life.

It was upon first "discovering" ledger-book art, published both in the Milwaukee Public Museum's folder titled *Sioux Indian Drawings* (1961), and later (1964) in the University of Oklahoma's *A Cheyenne Sketchbook* by Cohoe, that, in my innocence, I felt I could emulate the style of drawing. I was excited by its bright flat colors, its detail drawing, and Egyptian perspective. I had never had the confidence to draw people, but felt encouraged to try in the ledger-book style. (Ledger-book art is the name given to early Native American drawing, when pens and colored pencils were utilized for the first time, and traders' ledger-books were the only commonly available paper. Hence most examples of the genre are drawn on lined and numbered paper.)

I first visited the Little Bighorn Battle site in 1959, having already read several versions of the battle on June 25, 1876. I had just finished three years study in Furniture Design at the Central School of Arts and Crafts in London, and was spending the summer visiting Indian people, prior to starting work in furniture design in London. At the time I had no thought I would ever make a book. The visit to the battle site was in the company of three tall, strong Crow Indian men. In those days there were few visitors, and the guide, surely a little in awe of those three serious Crow men, gave a very fair account of the battle!

Back in England, almost ten years later, my young son, Richard, was watching a TV series about General Custer, which made out Custer to be a hero, which I knew he was not. I searched in the children's library and book shops for something to put the facts straight for my son, but found nothing. This was evidently the impetus I needed: to try to make a book myself, to use the voice of an Indian participant, and to illustrate the picture pages in the style of ledger-book painting. The book is dedicated to Richard.

Because no single Indian account gives a complete picture of the battle, Indian people telling only what they had seen and done, I added explanatory passages in italics to give the reader an overview of what might have taken place; there were no survivors of Custer's immediate command, and there has always been considerable controversy about exactly what happened.

It may be noticed that every two page spread of artwork takes three quarters of the spread, leaving room for a vertical column of text; in my inexperience of children's book making, I thought I was leaving sufficient space for columns of text for a fairly short book! My editor, the great children's book editor at Macmillan, London, Lady Marni Hodgkin, herself an American, quickly explained the impossibility of squeezing so much text into such small spaces! When the opportunity presented itself to produce this special edition of the book, I jumped at the chance. Its shorter page count and modified layout are closer to my original ideas for the book, and for the first time the illustrations are in glorious digitized color, scanned from the original artwork housed among the collections in the South Dakota Art Museum. I have also amended the text from the original edition to be slightly kinder to Major Reno, Custer's second in command. Initially, blame for the massacre fell on his shoulders, but with the benefit of historical hindsight, opinions are starting to change. The inclusion of the Foreword by Joe Medicine Crow, whose grandfather was Custer's own scout, White Man Runs Him, also gives the book a stronger Indian perspective.

I grew up believing that Indian people had been shamefully treated, their beliefs mocked, their ways of life destroyed. I tried to be objective in writing the book, but for me the battle represented a moment of triumph, and I wanted Indian children to be proud of it. In my mind, and translated into the illustrations, the soldiers wore shabby black hats, the Indians, beautiful white eagle feather war bonnets. I am an incurable romantic, and still rather see it like that. It should also be added that the late 1960s and '70s were times when Indian people sought to regain their pride. It was the time of the American Indian Movement (AIM), *Akwesasne Notes*, the sit-ins, the occupation of Wounded Knee, the Sun Dance and take-over of Wind Cave National Park, the Yellow Thunder Camp and the show trials of Dennis Banks and Russell Means. They were exciting times, and I admit that I saw the leaders in the image of their great warrior leader ancestors.

In the two previous editions of the book, I acknowledged the help of *Lakota Ishnala*, or Lone Sioux. This was Fr. Gall Schuon (1906-1991), a Trappist monk at the Abbaye Notre Dame de Scourmont in Belgium. Nicholas Black Elk (of the book, *Black Elk Speaks*) gave him the name and adopted him as his son. Father Gall spoke Lakota fluently and was steeped in all things related to Lakota people. While working on the book many letters passed between us to verify one thing or another. *Wopila ate.*

for Richard

"For a subject worked and reworked so often in novels, motion pictures, and television, American Indians remain probably the least understood and most misunderstood Americans of us all." John F. Kennedy

The Background

In early June 1876 the combined bands of the Lakota and their friends the Northern Cheyennes had celebrated their annual Sun Dance. Their leader, Chief Sitting Bull, on the fourth and final day of the dance, had received a vision of many soldiers and horses falling upside down into his camp. A few days afterwards the warriors led by Crazy Horse had defeated the soldiers of General Crook at the Battle of the Rosebud, but Sitting Bull knew that his vision promised a still greater victory.

In late June the Lakota and the Cheyennes had moved northward into the center of their last hunting grounds and were camped along the banks of the Little Bighorn River. They were not at war. This was one of their favorite valleys with abundance of wildlife and grass for their horses. Here they were happy and they wished to be left in peace with their women and children to pursue their own way of life.

However, the soldiers found their encampment. Sitting Bull's promised victory came on June 25 when General George Armstrong Custer and the Seventh U.S. Cavalry attacked his camp on the Little Bighorn River. It was the greatest victory ever won by American Indians. It was also one of the last battles fought in the unequal struggle which had started almost three hundred years before when white people first landed on American soil.

"I tell no lies about dead men. Those men who came with Long Hair were as good men as ever fought." Chief Sitting Bull

General Custer

George Armstrong Custer was a national hero of the Civil War with a reputation for reckless bravery. "Custer's Luck" was proverbial. He was an individualist. He designed his own uniforms and contrary to custom wore his hair long. In this campaign "Long Hair," as he was known to the Lakota, wore buckskins and a wide-brimmed hat, but his hair he had just cut short.

Future settlement of the West was blocked by the powerful Lakota and Cheyenne tribes. In 1876 General Sheridan was ordered by Congress to confine these tribes within reservations by military force. Sheridan's campaign plan was to converge troops from three directions simultaneously and force the Indians to fight. General Custer's advance was expected to form a link in this chain of forces which was to encircle the Indians. The plan was conceived on the false assumption that the Indians would flee and scatter rather than fight.

Custer had personal ambitions for this campaign. By forced marches he stole a lead on the other converging forces and led the Seventh Cavalry within striking distance of the Lakota and Cheyenne camps twenty-four hours ahead of schedule. Despite repeated warnings from his officers and Crow Indian scouts that the camp was too strong to attack without reinforcements, Custer would not listen. His only fear was that the Indians would elude him. The Indian wars were almost over and he hoped that by winning a final glorious victory he would one day be chosen as the nation's future president.

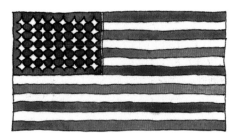

Red Hawk Begins

I am Oglala. I was fifteen winters old when Long Hair attacked our camp in the valley of the Little Bighorn. I was in that fight. We won a great victory. But when you look about you today you can see that it meant little. The White Men, who were then few, have spread over the earth like fallen leaves driven before the wind.

Today a railway stretches along the valley crossing the place where the circle of our tipis once stood. Beside the railroad there is a highway with many fast cars passing along it. White Men hurry from one place to another. They do not stop. They can make no money there and they see no beauty in the dry hills and the trees by the river. If they stop they only have eyes to read the writing on the graves and monuments. But walk away from the smell of the road and away from the noise of cars and radios and people and you will understand why Sitting Bull led us to that valley. It is beautiful. I remember how happy we always were there. The valley is the same today; men have changed but what the Great Spirit has made never changes.

The river winds along the valley, flowing silently through deep clear pools and bubbling fast over shallow stony bottoms. Cottonwood trees and red willow bushes grow along the banks and in the heat of summer all living things come there to enjoy the refreshing shade and the soothing sounds of the water and the rustling leaves.

Away from the river the earth is hard and dry, with sunflowers, sagebrush, and prickly pears growing. Here even a walking buffalo raises a dust.

We were strong then. And we were happy. I remember that our tipis were pitched in seven great circles beside the river where the valley bottom is flat. There were more tipis than could be counted. Our horse herds covered the sloping prairies to the west of the great encampment like cloud shadows. It was not often that the bands gathered because many people in one place frighten away the buffalo and too many horses soon eat off all the grass. I felt proud to see how many and how strong we were.

All the great chiefs were there. At the northern end of the encampment, close to a buffalo ford across the river, were our friends the Cheyennes led by young Two Moons. Next to them was a small band of Inkpaduta's Eastern Lakota driven far from their home by the soldiers. Then came the Sans-Arcs led by Chiefs Spotted Eagle and High Bear. Farther south, across Muskrat Creek, were the Miniconjous with their chiefs, Lame Deer and Touch-the-Clouds. They had a large circle opposite a second buffalo ford where a trail leads across the river and up two dry coulees which run back into the high hills. Just north of our circle was a small band of the Blackfoot Lakota under Fast Bull.

We, the Oglalas, had the largest circle in the encampment. Many famous men were with us that day and among them were He Dog, Little Hawk, Big Road, and Iron Shield, but the greatest of them all was Crazy Horse. He was more than a man. He was not a chief because he did not want honor for himself, yet no man ever won more honors and no man was more respected. Wherever he led, the people would follow. The White Men could never kill him in battle, but later, when we were at peace, they were still afraid of his power and he was taken from us to a soldiers' fort. He tried to fight his way out of that fort alone and he died with a soldier's bayonet in his back. But his spirit they could never kill. We remember him today.

Sitting Bull had his circle of Hunkpapas at the southern end of the encampment. Black Moon and Gall were with him. That summer Sitting Bull was chief over all the others and he led us to that valley to get away from the soldiers whom he knew were somewhere looking for our camp. Sitting Bull was no coward. But fighting is for warriors and his first thoughts were for the safety of the women and children.

The soldiers were closer than Sitting Bull realized. At dawn on June 25, Custer's Crow Indian scouts had climbed a high hill overlooking the valley. In the clear air just before sunrise they spotted the Lakota encampment fifteen miles to the north. Smoke was gently rising from hundreds of tipi fires through the mist which still lay in the bottom of the valley. Custer was some miles behind

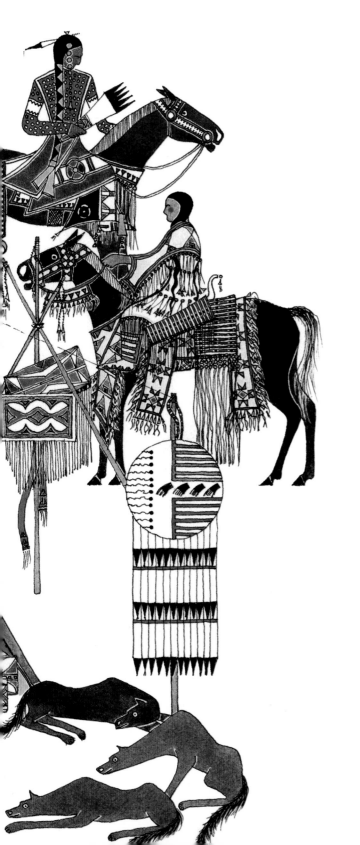

with the column and by the time he reached the hilltop the mist covered the valley like a blanket and nothing could be seen. "If we go in there we shall never come out," his scouts warned him. But Custer was jubilant. He completely ignored their warnings, telling them that their hearts were suddenly faint at the sight of their old enemies, the Lakota. Attack was foremost in his mind because, with "Custer's Luck," attack always meant victory. He divided his command. Major Reno was ordered to attack with three troops from the south, while he would attack with five troops from the east. Custer, bare-headed, knelt a moment in silent prayer. Mounting again he shouted, "Custer's Luck, boys! We've got them. We'll finish them off, then go home to our station. Come on!" The column advanced.

I do not remember now but I think that morning must have been like the others. I always woke to hear the birds greeting the dawn and saw the first rays of the rising sun shining on the smoke-flaps of the tipi above my head. My grandfather, Walking Elk, would rise first. Standing outside the doorway with his drum he joined his song with the birds to greet the returning sun. It was always so.

My father expected me to rise then. Our horses must be found and driven to the river to drink. Most of my friends would be with their horses too. We had to be careful not to let the horses kick up a dust around the tipis. If they did there were shouts from the women and sometimes it was fun to dodge the stones they threw at us.

It must have been when the sun had just passed its highest position in the sky. The heat in the valley was heavy and there was little movement in the encampment. The tipi-covers were rolled up at the bottom to catch any small breeze and the only sounds were the happy shouts and laughter of the children splashing in the river. I was with my father at the time, in Yellow Eagle's tipi at the northern edge of the Hunkpapa circle. Yellow Eagle was my uncle. He had just lit his long pipe with its polished red stone bowl. The women, bent over pale flames, were preparing food and the baby was hanging in his cradle from the tipi-poles, out of the sun. It was then that we first noticed it.

A long distance up the valley a dust cloud hung in the dancing haze which divided the sky from the prairie. It did not seem to be a cloud of approaching danger. It could have been raised by frightened stampeding buffalo or a sudden hot wind twisting dust from the hot earth.

But suddenly we heard the far-off sound of the bugle and underneath the cloud of dust there was steel flashing in the sun and a long thin line of blue separated from the haze.

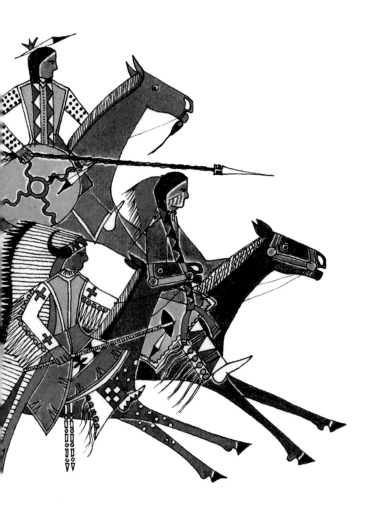

At once the cry went up: "Soldiers are coming! Horse-soldiers are attacking!" You could hear the cry going from camp to camp down the valley.

In an instant everyone was running in different directions. It was like an approaching thunderstorm when everyone runs to bring things in out of the rain and to set the tipi-flaps. But this was different, too. "Hurry! Hurry! Look after the children and the helpless ones!" The air was suddenly filled with dust and the sound of shouting and horses neighing. Dogs were running in every direction not knowing where to go. Boys ran to bring in the herds and the chiefs hurried from their tipis to help the frightened ones.

Warriors struggled to mount their horses, which reared and stamped in excitement, while women grabbed up their babies and shrieked for their children as they ran down the valley away from the oncoming soldiers. Old men and women with half-seeing eyes followed after, stumbling through the dust-filled air. Medicine Bear, too old to run, sat by his tipi as the bullets from the soldiers' guns already splintered the tipi-poles around him. "Warriors take courage!" he shouted. "It is better to die young for the people than to grow old."

I jumped on my horse and galloped to our tipi for my bow. My brother and little sister had already fled but my grandfather was there. He had braced my bow and was holding the quiver filled with the arrows which he had made for me. There was a look that I had not seen before in his eyes when

he handed them to me. I think he too wanted to go where the fighting was. "Take courage, grandson!" he said. "The earth is all that lasts." He tightened the rope around my horse's nose and I joined the stream of warriors galloping across the Hunkpapa circle to hold off the soldiers. But it was strange: the soldiers had stopped before reaching the camp and they were off their horses and shooting at us.

Black Moon and some other Hunkpapa warriors were whipping their horses up and down in front of the soldiers and raising a great dust to hide from view the women and children fleeing down the valley. They were brave men. Then Sitting Bull was there. "Warriors," he shouted, "we have everything to fight for, and if we are defeated we shall have nothing to live for, therefore let us fight like brave men." Even then we saw through gaps in the dust that the line of blue-coated soldiers was falling back to the shelter of the trees by the river. "Crazy Horse is coming! Crazy Horse is coming!" shouted the Oglalas sweeping down from the next camp.

"Crazy Horse is coming!" echoed the Hunkpapas, making way as he swept past us on his black horse painted with the white hail markings. A tomahawk in his hand gave him the power of the thunder and a war-bonnet of eagle feathers gave him the speed of the eagle. "*Hetchetu*! Be strong, my friends!" he shouted. "Remember the helpless ones!" With Crazy Horse leading, we all felt stronger; and with Black Moon and Gall there as well, we charged the soldiers.

Major Reno was frightened to advance farther when he saw the size of the Lakota encampment before him. By halting his troops he disobeyed Custer's orders and lost the advantage of surprise. As the warriors gathered in his front he was forced onto the defensive and withdrew to the timber beside the river to await Custer's attack. The soldiers with great superiority of firearms held their position, but Major Reno had never fought Indians before and he was unnerved by the ferocity of the Lakota attack.

The soldiers were well hidden among the trees close by where the river makes a big bend and they had many guns. The warriors in front charged up close to where the soldiers were and shot into the trees, but it was impossible to see what was happening in there. I saw my father and my uncle, Yellow Eagle, charging together once.

There was one brave Oglala with a war-bonnet and trailer of eagle feathers. I think it was Painted Thunder. I saw him gallop up alone to some bushes where a soldier was hiding and shoot into it. As he turned back towards us a white puff of smoke came from the bushes and his horse was shot. He jumped forwards as it went down and came back running, zig-zagging as he went, with his eagle feather trailer flying out behind him. It must have been the spirit of the eagle which saved him from the soldiers' bullets which were buzzing all around him. His medicine was strong that day.

Then suddenly everyone was shouting, "The soldiers are running! They are running!" and it was so. There was a line of soldiers galloping out of the trees farther up the river, running back from where they had come.

Hearing nothing from Custer and alarmed that he would be surrounded if he stayed longer where he was, Reno broke out from his position in panic, intending to rejoin Custer. Too late he realized his mistake. The soldiers' horses were tired with traveling since daybreak and within half a mile of leaving the safety of the trees the Lakota were abreast, forcing them back toward the river. The retreat became a rout. It was every man for himself in the dash across the open prairie to reach the high hills on the other side of the river.

"*Hoka Hey! Hoka Hey!*" It was like when the leader gives the sign to charge a herd of buffalo. At once everyone was shouting and all around me there was the shriek of eagle-bone whistles and the thunder of horses' hooves on the earth.

I whipped up my sorrel to keep beside my father and Yellow Eagle, but I soon lost them in the throng. Everywhere there was dust and everything moved in it like shadows in a dust storm. There were many ahead of me. I was riding close behind a warrior who had a shield slung across his back which flapped up and down as he galloped. There was red lightning painted on it with feathers fluttering from the center and I too felt the power and speed of the lightning.

And then I saw them. They were a short distance away on the side of our bows, bunched up close like frightened buffalo and running fast. "Hey! Hey! Hey! *Wasichu*!" I was excited. I had never seen soldiers so close before and they looked tall and strong on their big horses. Our bow-strings twanged and arrows flew like clouds of grasshoppers among their shadows, tumbling them from their saddles. I do not know if I hit any soldiers but I think I must have done. It was easy.

I saw Eagle Shield and Looks Twice range alongside a soldier with long hair on his cheeks and beat him across the back with their bows because it did not seem brave to kill him. But they killed him all the same, making the buffalo-killing cry as their arrows went through his body, "*Yi-hoo! Yi-hoo!*" It was more like chasing buffalo than fighting. It was the same with all the soldiers. They didn't turn to shoot because they were only thinking of running away. It went badly for them.

At the river it was worse. Their horses slid with stiff legs down the steep slope into the river.

I joined the warriors crowding there on the banks, shooting down at them all mixed up with their horses. It was terrible. It was like a sudden summer storm with a thunder and lightning of many guns and a darkness of dust and gun-smoke and bullets beating on the water like hailstones. Warriors jumped in as well to pull the soldiers from their saddles. They went under and came up again and again, floating down the river wrestling and fighting with knives and tomahawks. It was bad. Many died there in the river that day.

"*Henala*. It is enough. Let them go," cried Crazy Horse. And indeed it was. The soldiers had come to kill our women and children and we had driven them away. Many of them were dead and the rest were scrambling up the steep slopes across the river. "*Ho, hetchetu*; it is a great victory. My heart feels good," said Black Moon.

The Lakota harassed the soldiers on their difficult climb up the stony gullies leading to the top. There, exhausted, with nowhere else to go, the soldiers turned to fight. But twenty-nine soldiers and three officers lay dead in the valley below, while eighteen more were missing and of those surrounded on the hilltop many were wounded. Although utterly demoralized, the three hundred and twenty-five men left with Major Reno successfully defended their position.

Back a little way from the river my father was leading his horse with a body hanging across it. It was my uncle, Yellow Eagle. He was dead. He was my father's brother and my favorite uncle. Now he was dead. I think my father was too sad to speak. He just handed me a new six-shooter which he had captured from a soldier and a black leather pouch filled with shiny cartridges. That was my first six-shooter and I wanted to cross the river at once and to kill the soldiers because my uncle was dead.

But my father held me. It was not all. Even then warriors were streaming back down the river and a messenger was coming, his arm pointing back across the river towards the encampment. "More soldiers are attacking!" Where were the women and children? "Let a few stay here and watch those on the hill; the rest go against the new ones. Hurry! Hurry!"

We did not know how many more soldiers there were. Perhaps they were already killing the women and children as they had done to the Cheyenne on the Washita. What had become of my mother and my little sister? The way back to the camp seemed long. I wished then that my horse had wings as well as four legs, like the one Thunder Horse had painted on his tipi. This was indeed Sitting Bull's vision of many soldiers falling into the camp.

There was nobody in the Hunkpapa camp and the shooting was still farther up ahead, across the river.

But the helpless ones were safe. Above the shooting and the thunder of many horses galloping, we could hear them out on the low hills to the west making the tremolo to encourage us. They knew we had done a brave thing by driving back the first soldiers. I felt proud to hear them. We all shouted back and I held up my new six-shooter hoping that my mother and my little sister would see it.

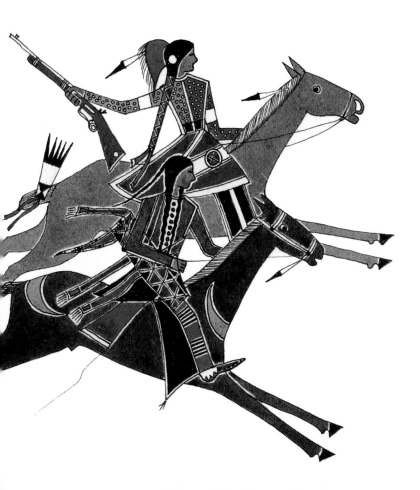

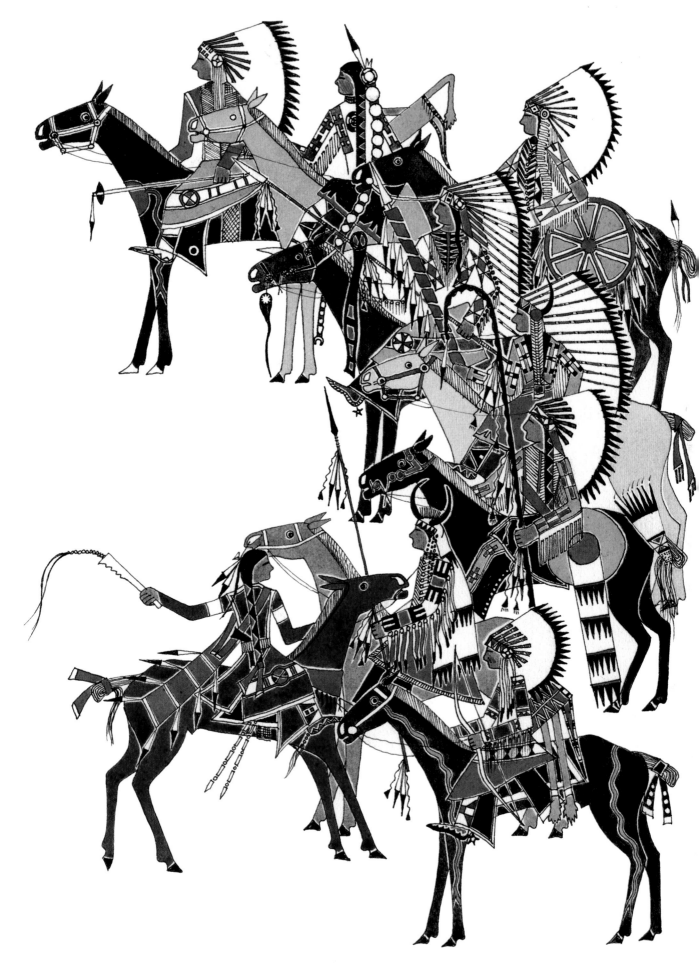

It was not until later that I heard how four brave Cheyennes and one Oglala had stopped the soldiers who came with Long Hair at the Miniconjou ford. Bobtail Horse, a Cheyenne, had just finished drilling a hole in an elk's tooth to tie in his hair for spirit-power when he saw soldiers, many soldiers, coming slowly down Medicine Tail Coulee. With Roan Bear, White Shield, Buffalo Calf, and the Oglala, White Buffalo Bull, he hid behind a bank close by the river and shot fast at the soldiers. They came on. Some fell from their saddles but the others still came on. They were not shooting nor did they stop to pick up their wounded as we would have done. Those five brave warriors shot fast to make the soldiers think there were many hiding behind the bank. The soldiers came on right to the ford and there, like the first soldiers, they stopped and got down from their horses. Why did they not cross? They were many against only five. All the way up the coulee they got down from their horses and formed into lines with some soldiers behind holding the horses. Then all together those nearest the river shot their guns with a sound like the tearing of a blanket by jerks. I heard that shooting too and knew it was the soldiers because only soldiers shoot like that.

When I reached the ford the soldiers had already climbed out of Medicine Tail Coulee and were going back up the hill. They went slowly, stopping to shoot back and then retreating up the slope again, falling as they went. They did everything slowly and together and nobody was excited, yet always they went back. Our Strong Heart Society warriors could not have fought harder and the soldiers died as bravely as they would have done. It was a hard struggle; very hard all the time. I have heard some White Men say that the soldiers were drunk and others say that the soldiers shot themselves. It is lies. The men who say that were never in the battle. Nobody can say those soldiers did not fight hard because I was there and I saw them. I never saw such brave men.

Of the two hundred and twenty-five men who rode down Medicine Tail Coulee with General Custer not one survived. It will never be known why he did not immediately cross the river to attack the camp. He did not know that Reno was already surrounded and it was possible that he was waiting for Reno to support him. It is also possible that he feared an ambush among the trees by the river and was unwilling to expose his troops to heavy fire while crossing the river. Victory might have been snatched with a bold charge through the encampment, but by waiting he gave the Indians time to collect on the opposite bank. After firing several volleys across the river in an effort to dislodge the Indians, he was soon forced by their determined attack to retire from the ford. The five troops of the Seventh U.S. Cavalry fell back up the slopes and Custer must have known that the only hope of survival for his command lay in reaching a defensive position on the ridge. From the time he left the ford until the last shot was fired it is probable that little more than twenty minutes passed.

It was an orderly retreat towards the ridge. Custer, with F, C, and E Troops in that order, retreated up the slope in echelon formation. E Troop, acting as rearguard, suffered the greatest casualties.

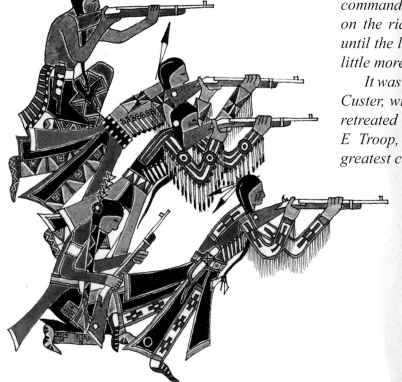

Then everyone was crossing the river and we whipped up our horses to join them. The water splashed up by the horses was cool on my body but there was no time to drink.

Custer divided his five troops, keeping C, E, and F under his immediate command. I and L Troops, under Captain Keogh, rode in columns of four up Deep Coulee, pursued by the Lakota led by Chief Gall. They climbed out of the coulee near its head and dismounted to meet the Indian attack. L Troop was overwhelmed at once and their bodies were later found in regular formation where they fell. Captain Keogh, with the remainder of I Troop, was cut down next as he attempted to rejoin Custer about a quarter of a mile away.

Suddenly Lame White Man, a Cheyenne chief riding next to me, fell backwards and I saw he had a hole through his chest with blood spurting from it. Red Shield helped me hold the chief in his saddle, but he was dead before we climbed out on the other bank. We dragged his body away from where the horses were crossing and then Red Shield fell as well. He was dead with a soldier's bullet through his head. He was terrible to look at. We were the same age and had always been friends.

There were two soldiers in a shallow draw just ahead and a little to one side, shooting from behind a dead horse. I was going to kill them. I sang the spirit song of the Hawk. The Hawk flies fast and the soldiers' bullets would not hit me. My horse knew how I felt and he was not frightened. It all happened fast. I took an arrow between my teeth and tightened another on my bow-string. One of the soldiers with red hair and a red face shot and missed. I hung low over my horse's neck but my arrow

went through his sleeve. I swung my bow as I passed to count coup but he dodged and my bow hit the other soldier's elbow. His gun went off at the same moment and I was blinded by the explosion and there was a taste of burnt powder in my mouth. I thought I had been hit. It was not until later that I found one of my braids almost cut in two. But I was happy; that was my first coup. I had touched an enemy and could now wear an eagle feather in my hair like a warrior.

The same soldier was up again and aiming at me as I turned. Again he missed, and my arrow went through his heart. He was young and I can still see him. The other soldier with the red hair was running up the slope looking back over his shoulder. He did not have time to turn because my arrow went right through him and he fell under my horse's hooves. Blood was coming out of his mouth and he was dead. Iron Star counted first coup. I took the six-shooter from my belt and shot the soldier again with many bullets. "That's for my uncle, Yellow Eagle!" and I shot again, "That's for Red Shield," and again, "That's for Lame White Man, the Cheyenne chief!" I guess I was pretty crazy, and scared, and angry too. Iron Star scalped him. It was the first time he had ever seen a man with red hair and he looked funny.

Suddenly there was a big thunder of hooves and people were shouting and there was a rush of horses galloping past us down the slopes like shadows through the dust. I thought at first the soldiers were charging. "The soldiers are running!" someone shouted. But it was not true. Our warriors were waving their blankets to frighten the soldiers' horses and they were stampeding. I wanted one of those big horses with its black saddle, like the one Brave Bear had taken at the battle on the Rosebud. I followed down the slope after a big black horse with a white star on his forehead. He was fast and I did not catch him until he was crossing the river. Then I grabbed the reins and crossed with him into the camp.

The dust had settled by then and the women and children were running back across the prairie to the camp. I gave the reins of the soldier's black horse to a boy to hold and I went back across the river. Afterwards I found many useful things in the saddle bags and at the bottom in a small bag there were many small pieces of green paper tied up with a

string which I threw away. I learned later it was money and I thought of all the things I could have bought with it at the White Man's fort.

Custer never reached the ridge. His retreat was impeded by the Lakota with Chief Black Moon pressing his left flank. The Indians, mostly dismounted, were fighting from prone positions behind every piece of cover and from small gullies leading towards the ridge. Custer was finally outflanked by Crazy Horse, and his troops were surrounded. Crazy Horse swept over the ridge in front of him and Custer, with no more than seventy men left, was forced to make his last stand just below the ridge. Today a cluster of white stones standing on the silent hillside marks the spot where those brave men fell.

The soldiers had gone back almost to the top. There were not many left and only a few puffs of smoke came from their guns. We did not know Long Hair was leading them; if we had known we would have fought even harder.

Our people had fought him many times before.

I left my horse and joined some warriors climbing up a shallow gulch. We could not see the soldiers from in there but their bullets passed close over our heads and one scattered dirt into my hair. I ran forwards and fell into a bed of prickly pear. Afterwards when my mother saw me she started to wail, thinking I had been wounded.

I had only been in the gulch a short time when we saw many horses coming down the ridge. "Crazy Horse is leading! It's Crazy Horse!" everyone was shouting and we ran up the slopes to join them circling round and round the soldiers, swirling like water round a stone. Suddenly one brave man charged across the circle and everyone followed, fighting with knives and tomahawks and empty guns for clubs. I saw Four Bears try to snatch a flag from a soldier's hands but he died full of soldiers' bullets.

Their flag must have been great medicine; the soldiers never let it touch the ground and when one soldier fell with it, another seized it again, until almost the last man was down.

When I reached that place the fighting was almost over. My memory now is clouded with the dust and noise and the smell of fighting. White Men have asked me which man it was who killed Long Hair. We have talked among ourselves about this but we do not know. No man can say. It was like a bad dream with horses and men all mixed up in fear and hate and I do not know what I saw then and what I saw in dreams later. I see men covered with blood and sweat and dust. I hear horses and men crying out in pain. I see brave things being done all around me and probably many more that nobody had time to see. I see wounded ones carried off by their friends to die or to get well again. I see, too, the frightened faces of babies and little children running from the soldiers' bullets. All these things I have seen and much more which is not for remembering again. It is enough. It was all over in the time it takes to light a pipe.

Red Hawk Ends

When I stood again on that ridge it was to meet the White Men as friends. Fifty winters had passed. It was in the year the White Men call 1926 that they called the Lakota and our friends the Cheyennes to a great gathering to remember the battle. There were old soldiers there who had fought in the first battle up the river with Major Reno, and many others whom we had fought in battles after that. There were many other important White Men there too, we were told, and they made long speeches which we could not understand. Soldiers in uniform blew on bugles, their way of remembering the dead, and they lowered their flag. Little Rock carried the flag for us and Chief Two Moons of the Cheyenne offered the pipe. He spoke a prayer to the Great Spirit and everyone stood there silent and alone in his remembering. I thought of my uncle, Yellow Eagle, and about the sadness there had been that night in his tipi.

I look back now and I see the battle need never have been. The long battle was over for us many winters before Long Hair ever came. We did not know the White Men were so many. We had seen the buffalo spread over the prairie and could see no end to them; the grasshoppers in summer cover the earth like a blanket and the wild duck in the spring and autumn fly in neverending lines. But the White Men are even more than these. Now the fighting between us is finished forever.

Once all the earth was ours; now there is only a small piece left which the White Men did not want. Our young men try to walk the difficult road of the White Men, and they remember with pride the example of our great chiefs Sitting Bull, Red Cloud, Crazy Horse and many others. They remember too with pride that we won a great victory that day by the Little Bighorn. It was so. I have spoken.

References

Information on the battle was taken from accounts appearing in the following books:

Grinnell, George B. *The Fighting Cheyenne*. Norman, Oklahoma: University of Oklahoma Press, 1956.

Hyde, George E. *Red Cloud's Folk*. Norman, Oklahoma: University of Oklahoma Press, 1937.

Marquis, Thomas B. *Wooden Leg*. Lincoln, Nebraska: University of Nebraska Press, 1957.

Miller, David H. *Custer's Fall*. London: Transworld Publishers Ltd, 1957.

Neihardt, John G. *Black Elk Speaks*. New York: William Morrow and Company, Inc., 1932.

————. *Eagle Voice*. London: Andrew Melrose, 1953.

Sandoz, Mari. *Crazy Horse*. New York: Alfred A. Knopf, Inc., 1942.

Stewart, Edgar I. *Custer's Luck*. Norman, Oklahoma: University of Oklahoma Press, 1957.

Vestal, Stanley. *Sitting Bull*. Norman, Oklahoma: University of Oklahoma Press, 1957.

For those who wish to know more about Sioux and Cheyenne ways, the following books are suggested:

Brown, Joseph E. *The Sacred Pipe*. Norman, Oklahoma: University of Oklahoma Press, 1953.

Cohoe, William. *A Cheyenne Sketchbook*. Norman, Oklahoma: University of Oklahoma Press, 1964.

Densmore, Frances. *Teton Sioux Music*. Bureau of American Ethnology, Bulletin 61, 1918.

Grinnell, George B. *The Cheyenne Indians*. New York: Cooper Square Publishers, Inc., 1964; Bloomington, Indiana: World Wisdom, 2008.

Hassrick, Royal B. *The Sioux*. Norman, Oklahoma: University of Oklahoma Press, 1964.

Laubin, Reginald and Gladys. *The Indian Tipi*. Norman, Oklahoma: University of Oklahoma Press, 1957.

Milwaukee Public Museum. *Sioux Indian Drawings*. Primitive Art Series No. 1.

Sandoz, Mari. *Cheyenne Autumn*. New York: McGraw-Hill, Inc., 1953.

Schmitt, Martin F. and Dee Brown. *Fighting Indians of the West*. New York: Charles Scribner's Sons, 1948.

Standing Bear, Luther. *My People, the Sioux*. Boston: Houghton Mifflin Company, 1928.

————. *My Indian Boyhood*. Boston: Houghton Mifflin Company, 1931.

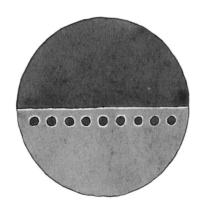